Patchwork

Family

Written by Felicia Law
Illustrated by Paula Knight

NORWOODHOUSE PRESS

Chicago, Illinois

DEAR CAREGIVER   The **Patchwork** series is a whimsical collection of books that integrate poetry to reinforce primary concepts among emergent readers. You might consider these modern-day nursery rhymes that are relevant for today's children. For example, rather than a Miss Muffet sitting on a tuffet, eating her curds and whey, your child will encounter a Grandma and Grandpa dancing a Samba, or a big sister who knows how to make rocks skim and the best places to swim.

Not only do the poetry and prose within the **Patchwork** books help children broaden their understanding of the concepts and recognize key words, the rhyming text helps them develop phonological awareness—an underlying skill necessary for success in transitioning from emergent to conventional readers.

 As you read the text, invite your child to help identify the words that rhyme, start and end with similar sounds, or find the words connected to the pictures. The pictures in these books feature illustrations resembling the technique of torn-paper collage. The artwork can inspire young artists to experiment with torn-paper to create images and write their own poetry.

Above all, the most important part of the reading experience is to have fun and enjoy it!

Sincerely,

Shannon Cannon

Shannon Cannon, Ph.D.
Literacy Consultant

Norwood House Press • P.O. Box 316598 • Chicago, Illinois 60631
For more information about Norwood House Press please visit our website at
www.norwoodhousepress.com or call 866-565-2900.

LIBRARY OF CONGRESS CATALOGING-IN-PUBLICATION DATA
Law, Felicia.
  Family / by Felicia Law ; illustrated by Paula Knight.
     pages cm. -- (Patchwork)
  Summary: Torn paper collages and simple, rhyming text portray children interacting with family members, from
Uncle Ray who teaches one about cars, to grandparents who love to go dancing. Includes a word list.
   ISBN 978-1-59953-711-5 (library edition : alk. paper) -- ISBN 978-1-60357-809-7 (ebook)
[1. Stories in rhyme. 2. Families--Fiction.] I. Knight, Paula, illustrator. II. Title.
   PZ8.3.L3544Fam 2015
   [E]--dc23
                                        2014047195

274N—062015
Manufactured in the United States of America in North Mankato, Minnesota.

Three cousins

When my aunt and uncle
come for the day
They bring my cousins
and we all play
Up on the hillside
having some fun
Left to ourselves till the
grown-ups come!
'Don't be so noisy' someone will call
'I really don't know
what gets into you all!
It sounds like an army
is going to war.'
But making a noise
is what cousins are for!

3

My Uncle Ray

My Uncle Ray
fixes cars all day
And when he's not busy
He shows me the way
the engine roars
And the button you press that
opens the doors
The windshield wipers
that swish to and fro
And the light on the dashboard
that makes it glow

5

Dad

Dad says
   he wants a bit of peace

All he wants to do is
   drink a mug of tea
   kick off his shoes
   pat the cat and dog
   and read the football news

And then – he says
   he'll be free
And then – he says
   he'll play with me

7

My little sister

My little sister
is a horrid horrid child
She's noisy
and a nuisance
She's messy
and she's wild

She throws tantrums
and she teases
She pesters me all day

And Mom agrees she's naughty
But still she gets her way!

My cousin

My cousin is so grown up
When she's chatting to her friend
About her favorite pop star
And her plans for the weekend

About her newest lipstick
And she's trying not to be
My babysitter cousin ...
With no time to talk to me!

11

Grandma and Grandpa

On Saturday nights
My grandma and grandpa
Go dancing
They take hours to dress and then
They go prancing

Twirling to the music
They waltz and they quickstep
They foxtrot and they samba
My grandma and grandpa

14

Mommy

My Mommy
Says inside her is Tommy
My baby brother
all curled up like a ball

She says he's very little
with tiny hands and toes
He's staying warm
   inside her

While he grows and grows and grows

Aunt Sarah

Aunt Sarah's always cooking
Particularly cakes
She's often in the kitchen
Where she bakes and bakes and bakes

She says that I can help her
Scrape the bowl and lick the spoon
And would I like to join her
For tea that afternoon?

Granny Peg

Granny Peg sows lots of seeds
She plants them in the ground
She waters them each morning
And weeds the soil around

Then little baby shoots appear
Tall stalks and leaves of green
And petals bloom to make
The nicest flowers ever seen

19

Big brother

My big brother
is the best
skateboarder
you will find

He does an 'ollie' and a 'nollie'
A 'kickflip' then a 'grind'
A 'heelflip' and a 'fakie'
A 'big spin', a 'wall ride'
A 'half-cab' and a 'blow-out'
A 'nose grab' and a 'slide'

This book includes these concept words:

- afternoon
- aunt
- baby
- brother
- car
- cousin
- dad
- day
- dog
- door
- engine
- flower
- friend
- grandma
- grandpa

- grown-up
- kitchen
- mom
- morning
- mug
- music
- play
- seed
- sister
- soil
- spoon
- sports
- tea
- uncle